Who's Been Eating MY Porridge?

For Megan

Scholastic Children's Books
Euston House, 24 Eversholt Street
London, NW1 1DB UK
A division of Scholastic UK Ltd

London ~ New York ~ Toronto ~ Sydney ~ Auckland
Mexico City ~ New Delhi ~ Hong Kong

First published in hardback in the UK by Scholastic UK Ltd, 2003
First published in paperback in the UK by Scholastic UK Ltd, 2003
This paperback bind-up edition first published in the UK by Scholastic UK Ltd, 2005

Copyright © Nick Ward, 2003

ISBN 0 439 95057 0

Printed in Singapore

Papers used by Scholastic Children's Books are made from wood grown in sustainable forests

Who's Been Eating MY Porridge?

Nick Ward

Early one morning, Little Bear
woke up with a rumble in his
tummy. He crept downstairs
as quietly as he could, but . . .

. . . when he got to the kitchen, the porridge pot was nowhere to be seen. "That's strange," said Little Bear. "Mama always leaves it ready for breakfast."

Just then, there was a
knock at the door.
Little Bear lifted the latch,
and there stood . . .

. . . Little Billy Goat Gruff.
"Quick, let's run," bleated
Billy. "It can't have gone far!"

"What do you mean?" asked Little Bear.
"The Porridge Monster!" cried Billy.
"Look!" and he pointed to . . .

. . . huge porridgey footsteps leading
out of the door.
"It's taken our porridge pot, too,"
explained Billy. "Come on!"

So Little Bear and Billy set off to find their porridge.

They hadn't gone far when they met Little Miss Muffet.

"Have you seen our porridge?" asked the two friends. "The Porridge Monster took it!"

"No, but you can share my curds
and whey," said Little Miss Muffet.
Little Bear's tummy rumbled.
"Yes please," he said, just as . . .

KERPLOP! A big hairy spider jumped into Little Miss Muffet's bowl.
"Eeeek!" cried everyone, and away they ran, over the hills and down the lane, until they came to . . .

. . . Jack's house.
"Have you seen our porridge?"
asked Little Bear and Billy. "The
big hairy Porridge Monster took it!"
"No, but you can have some
beans," said Jack.
Little Bear's tummy rumbled.
"Well," he began, when . . .

Invitation

Thump! Thump! Thump!

An enormous boot appeared at the top of the beanstalk.

"It's the giant!" yelped Jack. "Run!"
And Little Bear and Billy and Little Miss Muffet and Jack ran and ran, through the field and up to the forest, where they met . . .

. . . Little Red Riding Hood.
"Have you seen our porridge?" panted
Little Bear and Billy. "The giant hairy
Porridge Monster took it!"
"No," said Little Red Riding
Hood. "But you can have
some jam."

Where did everyone go?

To Grandma's

Little Bear's tummy
rumbled.
"Yummy!" he said,
but then . . .

. . . a terrible howling came from deep within the forest.

"It's the big bad wolf!" cried Little Red Riding Hood. "Run!"

And off they all ran, through the forest and down to the stream, straight into . . .

. . . the Three Bears, who were coming home from holiday. "Have you seen our porridge?" gasped Little Bear and Billy. "The giant, hairy, howling Porridge Monster took it!"

It was only me!

"No, but you are
welcome to join us
for breakfast, dears,"
said Mother Bear.
Little Bear's tummy
rumbled.
"Thanks," he said,
when suddenly . . .

"Look!" cried Billy. "The footsteps are back!"
"Hmmm," said Father Bear. "They seem to be leading to . . .

. . . *my* house!"

Little Bear shivered.
"It must be . . ."

Everyone held their breath as Mother Bear reached for the door.

Slowly she turned the handle.
"Come on out, whoever you are!"
she cried, and she flung open the door
to find . . .

Dear Jack
Please come to an amazin[g]
Porridge Party
welcome home

Dear Little Red Riding Hood
Please come to an amazing
Porridge Party
to welcome home
The Three Bears
P.S. I've borrowed your Porridge Spoon!
7.00 a.m.   3 Bears Lane   love Goldilocks X

Dear Little Billy Goat Gruff
Please come to an amazing
Porridge Party
to welcome home
The Three Bears
P.S. I've borrowed your Porridge Pot!
love Goldilocks X
[...] Bears Lane

They all went out and played 'til bedtime!
"That was fun!" said Wolfie afterwards.
"Come again soon!" said Little Bear.

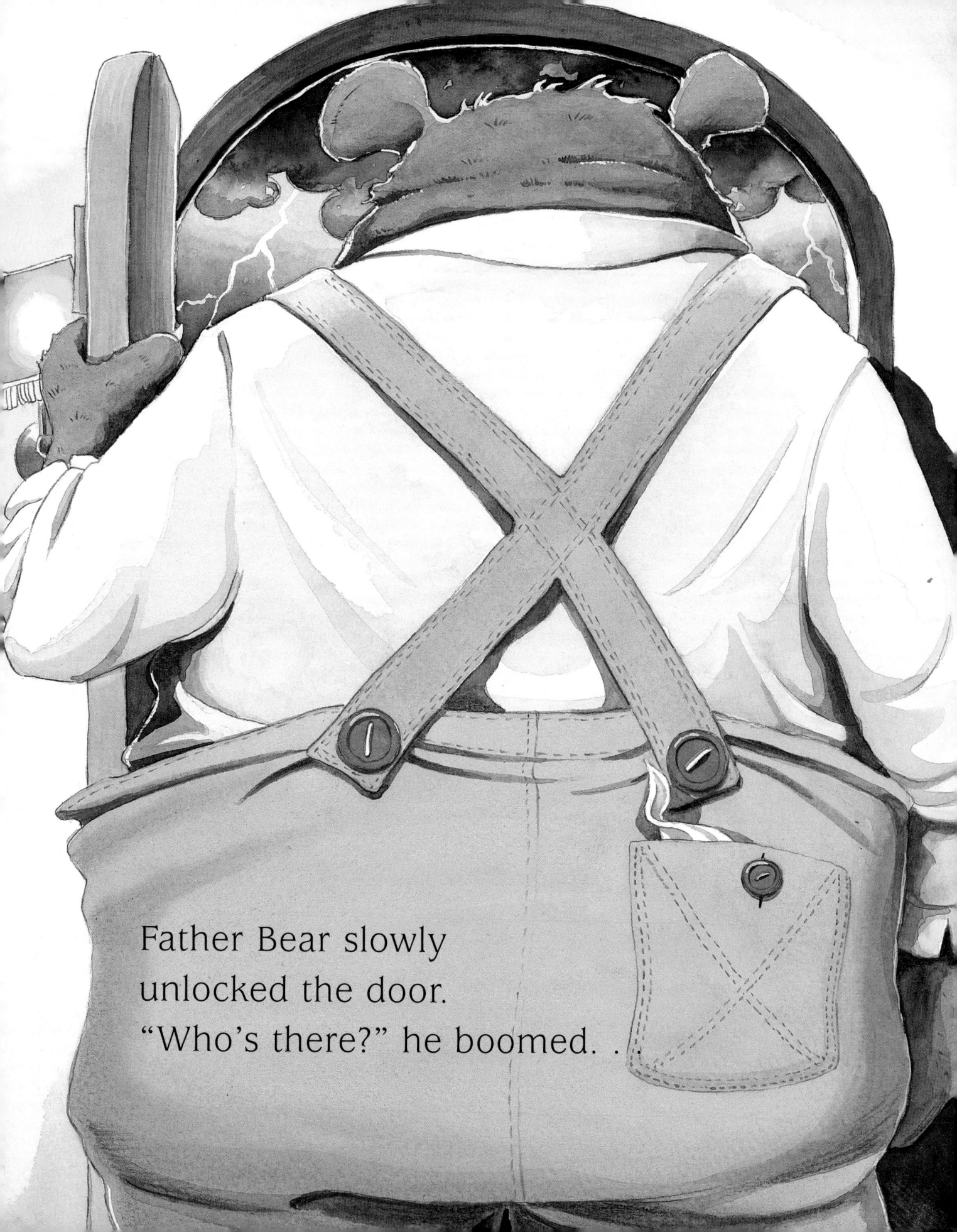

Father Bear slowly
unlocked the door.
"Who's there?" he boomed. . . .

Just then, **KNOCK! KNOCK!** went the door.
The house . . . went . . . very . . .
very . . . quiet.

Father Bear came in from the yard. "Goodness," he gasped. "What are all your friends doing here?"

"They've escaped from a terrible wolf," said Little Bear.

So Little Bear sat them all down and started to read his story. But he kept being interrupted by a **Knock! Knock!** at the door.

First there was Little Red Riding Hood,

then Cinderella,

and finally Goldilocks.

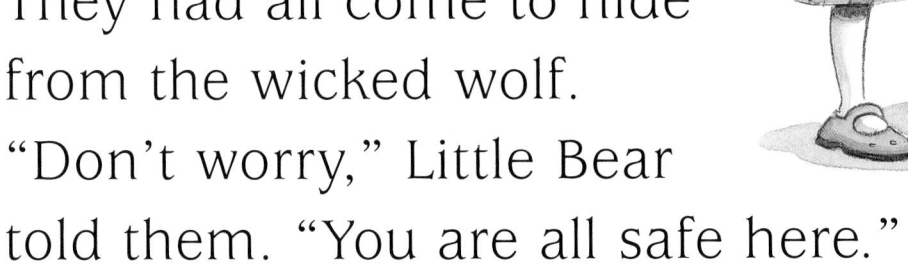

They had all come to hide from the wicked wolf. "Don't worry," Little Bear told them. "You are all safe here."

"We ran for our lives," chorused the
sheep. "But he chased us!"
"We could hear him panting."
"We could feel his hot, wolfie breath."
"He was huge," baaed the sheep.
"He was fierce and angry," piped
the pigs.
"He was lean and mean," bleated Billy.
"And we didn't stop 'til we got to your
door," finished Bo Peep.

"Down in the field," panted Bo Peep. "I heard the hedge rustle and I saw his bushy tail. And he bellowed . . ."

. . . Little Bo Peep and all
her sheep!
"Lock the door," cried Bo Peep.
"A wolf is after us!"
"What happened?" asked
Little Bear, as he locked the
door, quickly.

KNOCK! KNOCK! went the door!
"Who's there?" called Little Bear.
"It's Bo," said a voice.
"Please let me in."

Little Bear lifted
the latch, opened
the door and
in rushed . . .

"Don't worry," said Little Bear. "You're safe here." And he sat them down to listen to the story. All was quiet and calm, when . . .

"We left our house and ran and ran, 'til we got to your door," squealed the three pigs.

Little Bear let them in and locked the door.

. . . the three little pigs!
"Lock the door, quickly!" they cried.
"A huge wolf is after us! He came
to our house and he roared,
'Come out, come out, wherever you
are!' He was fierce. He was angry!"
"And he was lean and mean,"
added Billy.

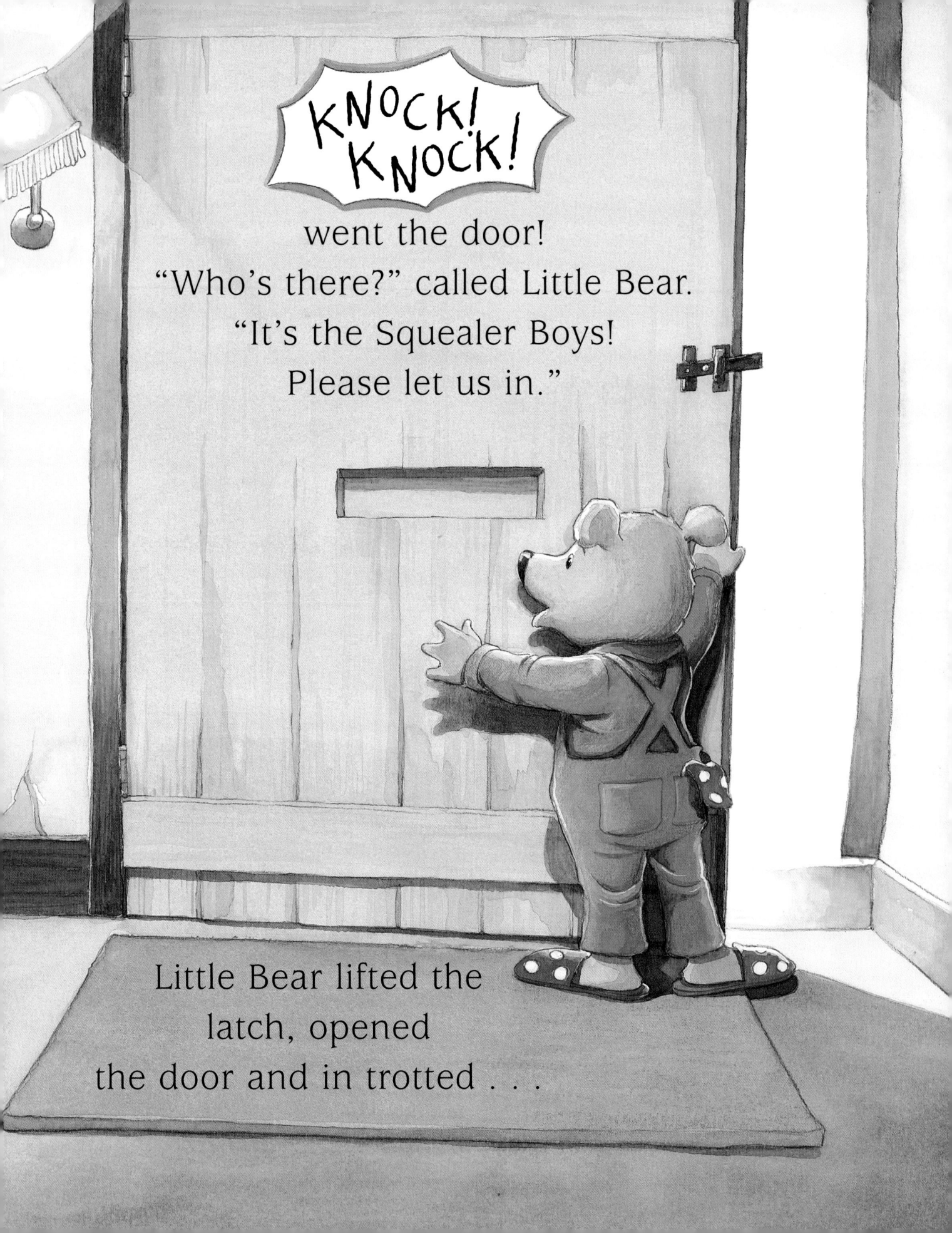

KNOCK! KNOCK!

went the door!
"Who's there?" called Little Bear.
"It's the Squealer Boys!
Please let us in."

Little Bear lifted the
latch, opened
the door and in trotted . . .

Little Bear sat Billy down.
"Don't worry," he said. "You're safe here."
And he started to read Billy a story.
All was cosy and quiet, when . . .

"I saw him up on the mountain," the little goat whimpered. "I saw his long, black shadow. He looked lean and mean, so I ran and ran 'til I got to your door!"

. . . Little Billy Goat Gruff!
"Lock the door, quickly!" bleated
Billy. "A wolf is after me! And he
shouted, 'Come out, come out,
wherever you are!'"

"It's Billy," a tiny voice bleated. "Please let me in." Little Bear lifted the latch, opened the door and in trotted . . .

Knock! Knock! went the door.
"Who's there?" asked Little Bear,
jumping down from his chair.

One quiet afternoon, while Father Bear
was in the yard chopping wood, Little
Bear sat reading his favourite book.
All was cosy and peaceful, when . . .

A WOLF at the DOOR!

Nick Ward

For Rob O'Connor

Scholastic Children's Books
Euston House, 24 Eversholt Street
London, NW1 1DB UK
A division of Scholastic UK Ltd

London ~ New York ~ Toronto ~ Sydney ~ Auckland
Mexico City ~ New Delhi ~ Hong Kong

First published in hardback in the UK by Scholastic UK Ltd, 2001
First published in paperback in the UK by Scholastic UK Ltd, 2002
This paperback bind-up edition first published in the UK by Scholastic UK Ltd, 2005

Copyright © Nick Ward, 2001

ISBN 0 439 95057 0

Printed in Singapore

Papers used by Scholastic Children's Books are made from wood grown in sustainable forests

A WOLF at the DOOR!